This hug belongs to:

....

FREE
HUGS

We Love You, Mr Panda

Steve Antony

FREE
HUGS

I need a hug.

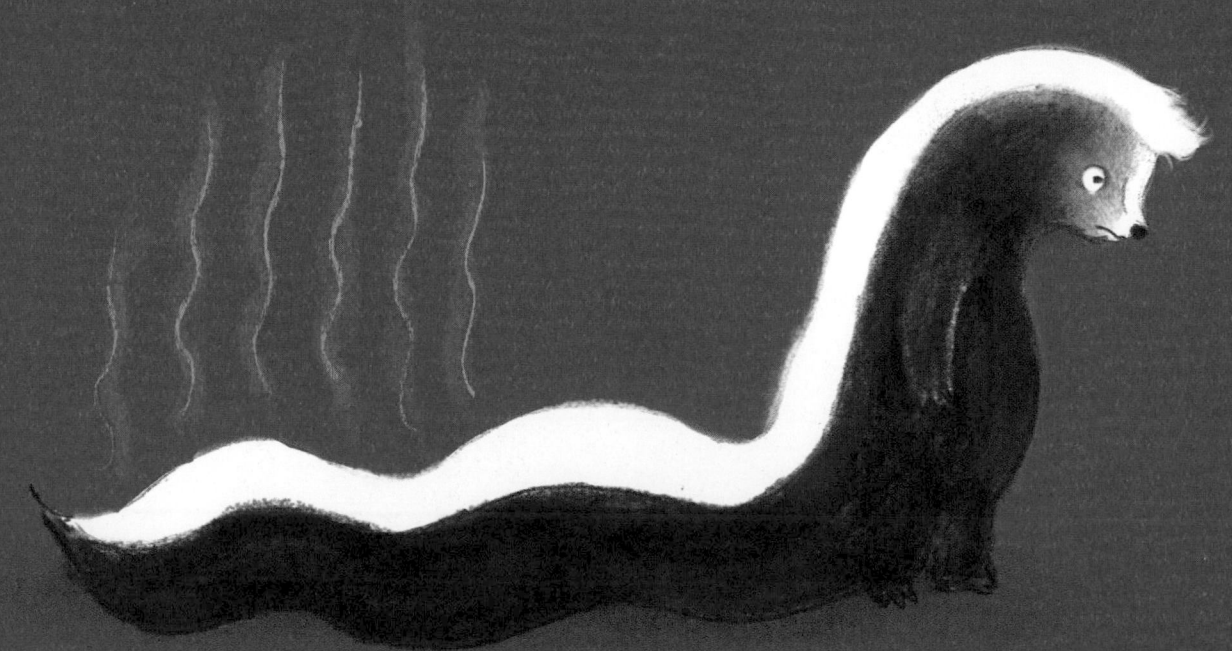

OK, Skunk. Let's have a hug.

FREE
HUGS

FREE
HUGS

I love you, too.

I was talking to Croc.
I love you, Croc.

May I please have a hug?

OK, Elephant. Let's have a hug.

I was talking to Mouse. I love you, Mouse.

I love you, too.

Would you like a hug, Sloth?

FREE
HUGS

No thanks, Mr Panda.
I can hug myself.

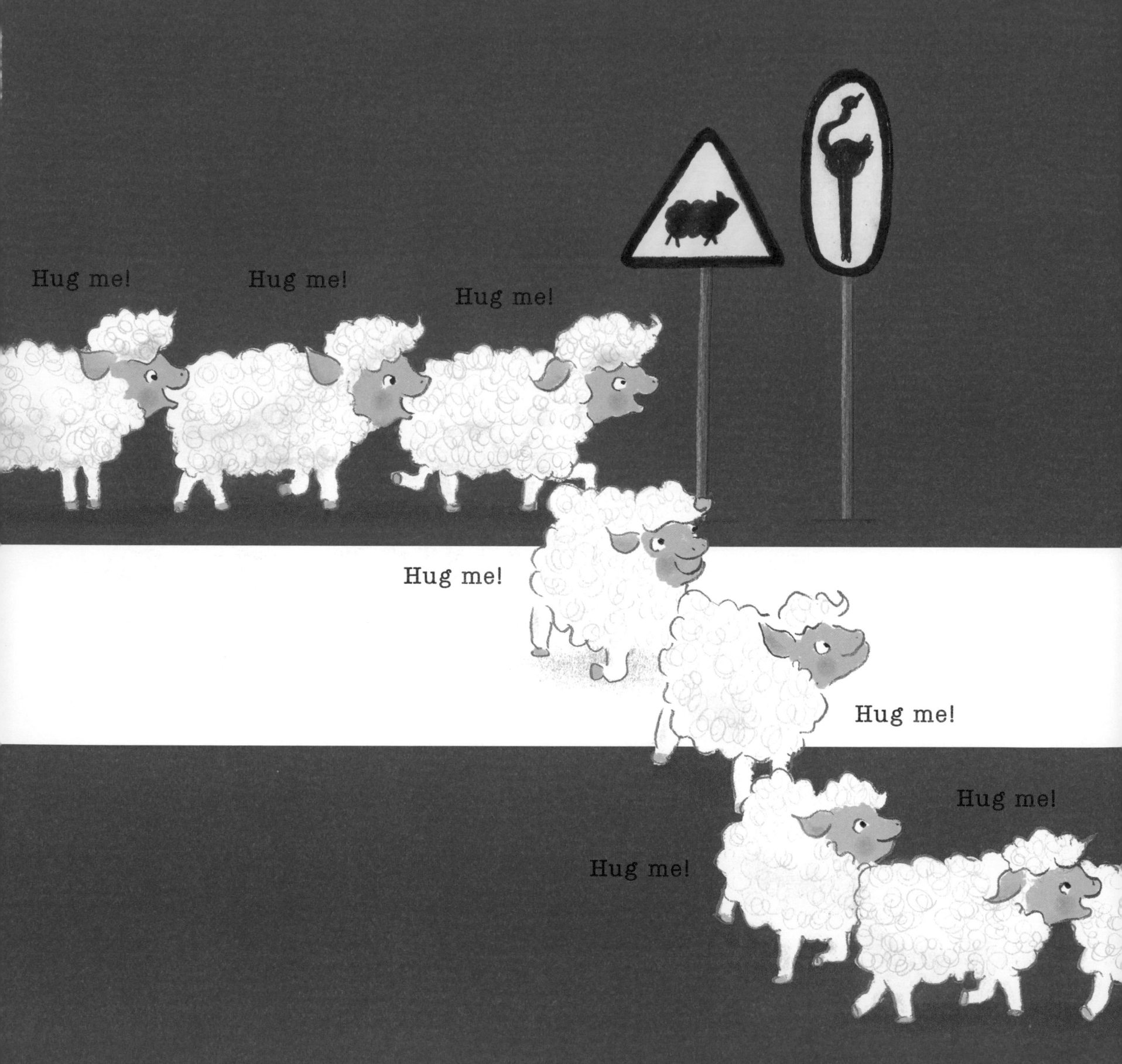

OK, sheep. Let's have a hug.

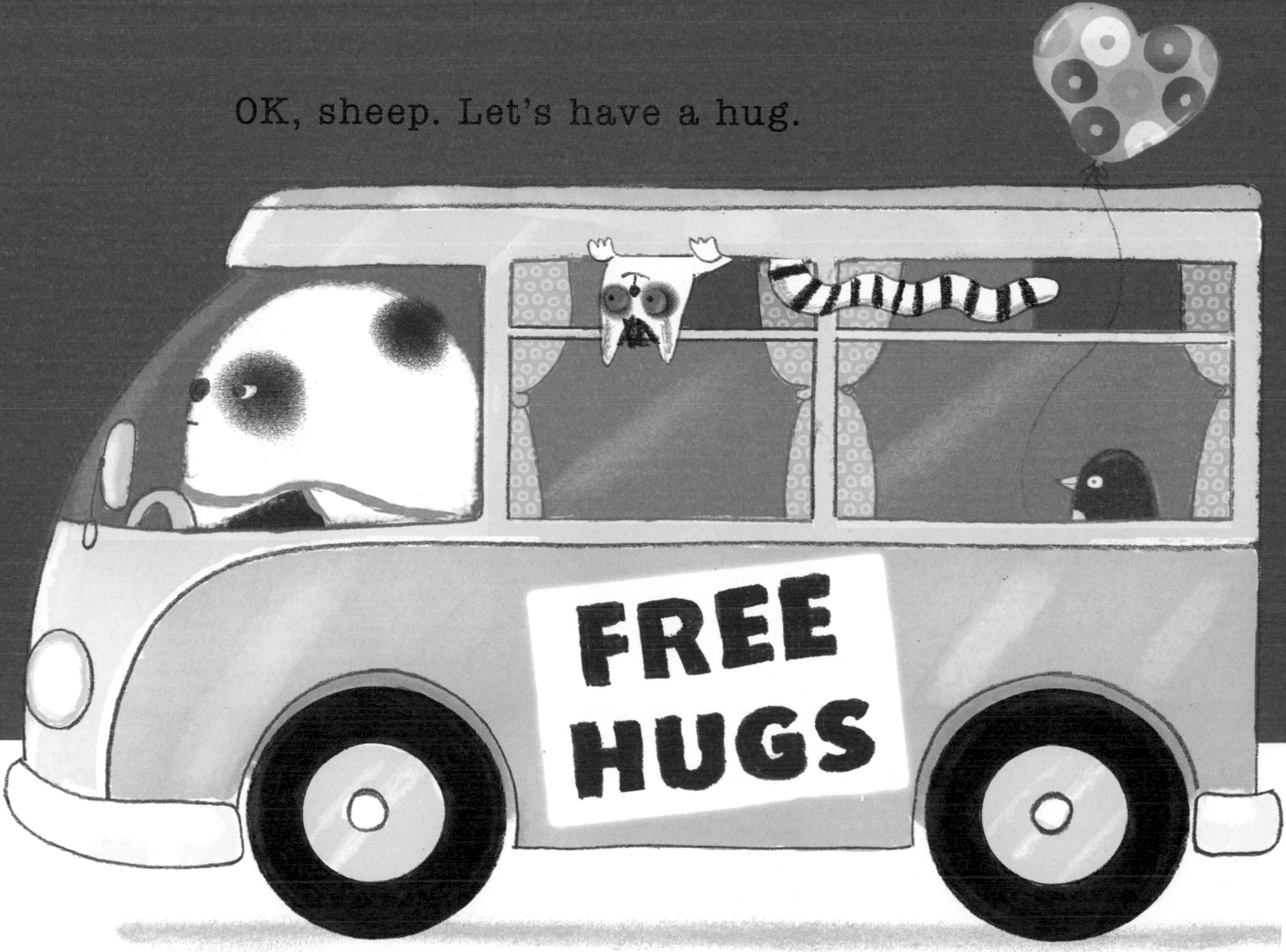

Hug me! Hug me! Hug me! Hug me! Hug me! Hug

We were talking to Ostrich.
We love you, Ostrich.

I love you all, too.

I guess nobody

wants my hugs . . .

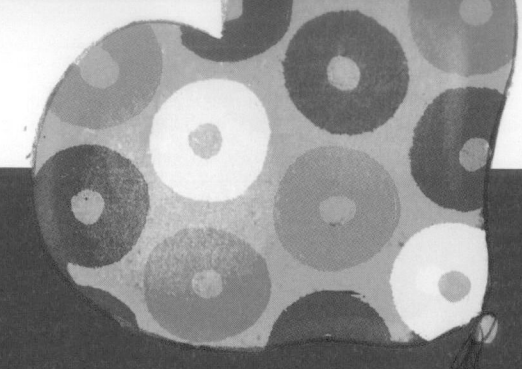

Don't go, Mr Panda.

Would YOU like a hug?

No, I would not like a hug . . .

. . . I would LOVE a hug. Thank you.

And so would we!

We love you, Mr Panda!

I love you, too.

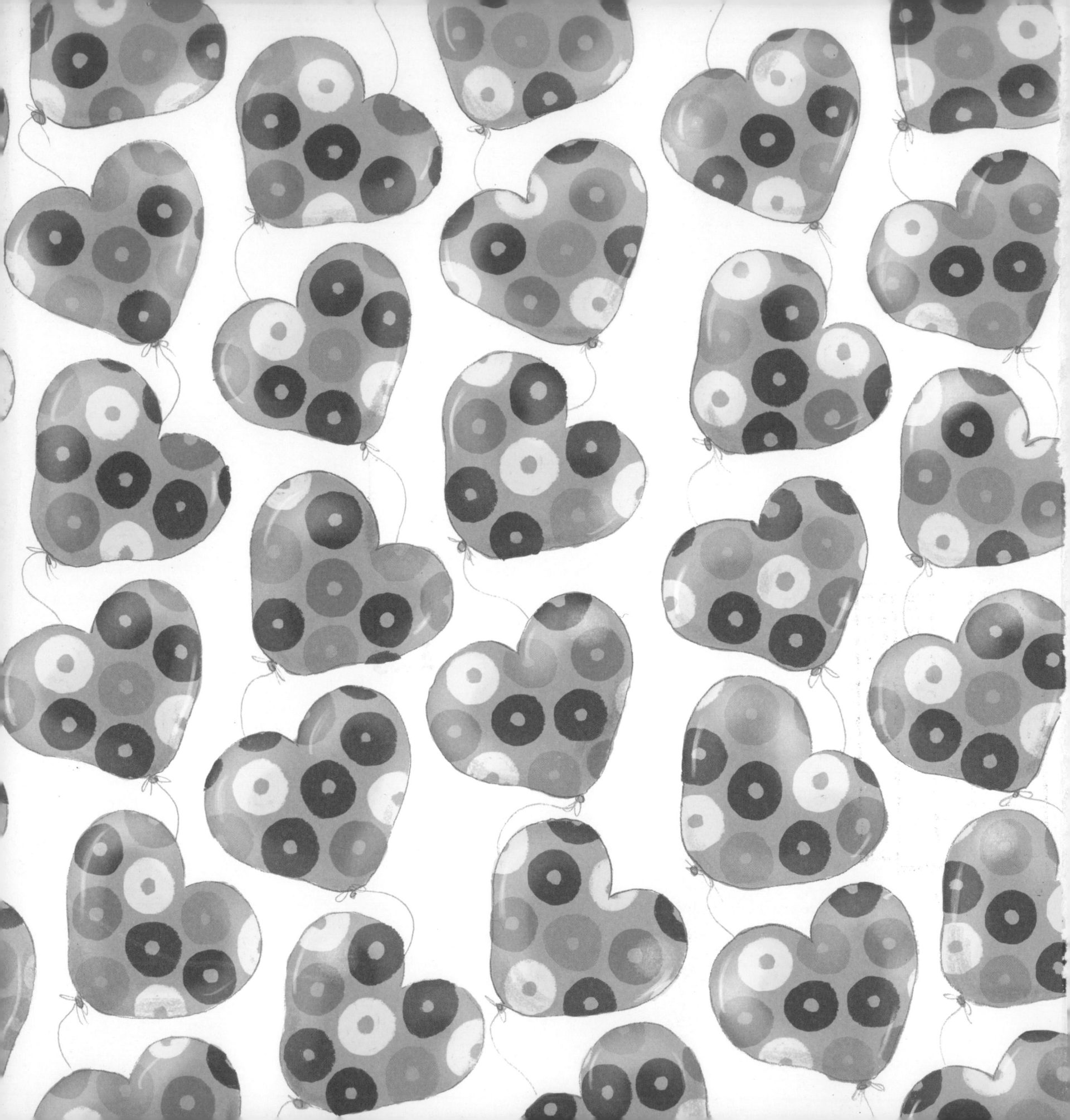

Also by Steve Antony:

I'll Wait, Mr Panda
Steve Antony

Goodnight, Mr Panda
Steve Antony

...You, Mr Panda
Steve Antony

Please Mr Panda
Doughnuts
Steve Antony

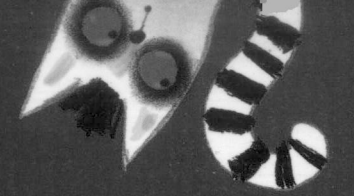

Mr Panda is ready for some hugs –
and he's giving them out for free!
But his friends are too busy hugging each other...

Does no one love Mr Panda?

FREE HUGS

Praise for *Please Mr Panda*:
'An ideal book for kids to learn about
the importance of good manners.' *Sun*

ISBN 978-1-44492-792-4

FSC

9 781444 927924

Hodder
Children's
Books

£8.99

hachettechildrens.co.uk